D1745195

Celtic Tales
OF
Enchantment

LIAM MAC UISTIN

Illustrated by Ruiséal Barnett

THE O'BRIEN PRESS
DUBLIN

First published 2001 by The O'Brien Press Ltd,
20 Victoria Road, Dublin 6, Ireland.
Tel: +353 1 4923333; Fax: +353 1 4922777
E-mail books@obrien.ie
Website www.obrien.ie

ISBN: 0-86278-692-4

British Library Cataloguing-in-Publication Data
A catalogue record for this title is available from the British Library

1 2 3 4 5 6 7 8 9
01 02 03 04 05 06 07

The O'Brien Press receives
assistance from

the**arts**
council
an chomhairle
ealaíon
50৳

Editing, typsetting, layout and design: The O'Brien Press Ltd.
Illustrations: Ruiséal Barnett
Cover separations: C&A Print Services Ltd.
Printing: Cox & Wyman Ltd.

CONTENTS

For my Niamh Cinn Óir
and for Paul,
her gallant Oisín

CelTic TaLes of EnchanTmenT

Praise for Liam Mac Uistin's Classic Celtic Tales Series:

'This is the answer for those children who think
Irish legends are boring'
IRISH GUIDE TO CHILDREN'S BOOKS
'A magical read'
IRISH INDEPENDENT
'A collection to stir any heart'
SUNDAY PRESS
'Magical stuff and a perfect gift'
EDUCATION MATTERS
'A sweeping, colourful narrative that grips
the interest of all readers'
LEINSTER LEADER

LIAM MAC UISTIN is a Celtic scholar, writer and playwright. One of his writings was selected by the Irish government for inscription in the National Garden of Remembrance in Dublin.

Celtic Tales of Enchantment is his fourth book of ancient Celtic tales. *The Táin*, his acclaimed version of the epic Táin Bó Cuailgne (The Cattle Raid of Cooley), has introduced many young readers to one of Ireland's most enduring legends. Liam is also the author of a non-fiction title, *Exploring Newgrange*, which provides a fascinating introduction to the history of this ancient megalithic site.

PROLOGUE

As in my previous books of stories from the fascinating world of Celtic legend, *Celtic Tales of Enchantment* contains exciting and entertaining tales of magic and wonder from the rich store of Celtic lore.

Like most of the old stories from Celtic mythology, these tales were passed on by storytellers from one generation to another. Later, they were written down by scribes in monasteries and in other places of learning.

The stories in this book are all about the legendary Fionn Mac Cumhaill and the Fianna, the army which had been formed under his command to defend the High King and the land of Ireland. The Fianna were at the height of their power during the reign of the celebrated High King, Cormac Mac Airt.

Fionn, the son of the great warrior Cumhall, had his main fortress on the Hill of Allen, near Newbridge in County Kildare. The Fianna comprised different tribes or clans, each under its own commander but subject to the overall command of Fionn. The most powerful of these clans were Clann Baoiscne of Leinster, commanded directly by Fionn, and Clann Morna of Connacht, under the immediate command of Goll Mac Morna.

Apart from Fionn Mac Cumhaill, the most important members of the Fianna were Fionn's son, Oisín, and his grandson, Oscar; Diarmaid Ó Duibhne; Goll Mac Morna, his brother Conán (noted for his gluttony, his boasting and his venomous tongue); and Fionn's nephew, Caoilte Mac Rónáin, who was famed for his fleetness of foot.

'The Enchanted Palace' recounts the gripping tale of *Brúíon Caorthainn* (The Palace of the Quicken Trees), one of the most exciting of all the adventures of Fionn Mac Cumhaill and his intrepid band of warriors. It relates how Fionn and his comrades are lured into a deadly trap by the treachery and the magic of their enemies.

'The Quest for the Giolla Deacair' is a humorous account of the enchantment of Conán Mac Morna and other Fianna stalwarts by the Giolla Deacair, a Tuatha Dé Danann magician in disguise.

'Oisín and Niamh Cinn Óir' is one of the most romantic and best-known stories about the Fianna. It tells of the love of Fionn's son, Oisín, for the beautiful Niamh of the Golden Hair, how he follows her to the Land of Eternal Youth, Tír na nÓg, and the strange fate that awaits Oisín when he returns to Ireland many years later.

In 'Ailne's Revenge', the widow of the King of Iceland conspires with her brother, the giant and magician Draoiantóir, to lure Fionn and the Fianna to their deaths in revenge for the killing of her husband and nephews at the bloody battle of Cnoc an Áir.

These lively and dramatic tales take the reader into an enthralling world of heroism, revenge, love, betrayal and magic.

Che eNCHANCED PALACe

The horse thundered over the plain of Kildare, white flecks of sweat beading its flanks and its flying hooves sparking like flints off the stony track. And still the rider spurred his steed on to greater speed. Just as it reached the high gates of the great fort on the Hill of Allen, the exhausted animal collapsed on the ground, throwing the rider in a somersault over its head.

He scrambled to his feet, ran to the gates and beat frantically on them with his fists. 'Open up!' he shouted. 'I have an urgent message for Fionn Mac Cumhaill.'

A peep-hole slid open in a wooden panel and a pair of eyes surveyed him warily. 'Where are you from?' the sentry demanded.

'I have been sent by the High King in Tara. I must see Fionn Mac Cumhaill at once!'

The gates swung open and a tall warrior motioned to

the messenger to follow him, at the same time ordering a servant to tend to the gallant horse. The warrior led him into the great hall of the fort, where Fionn Mac Cumhaill, the leader of the Fianna, was talking to his son, Oisín, and his grandson, Oscar.

'A messenger from the High King,' the warrior announced.

Fionn beckoned the messenger over. 'What news do you bring from the noble Cormac Mac Airt?'

'He sent me to tell you that we are all in great danger. A huge fleet of ships has arrived from the land of Lochlann and deposited an army on our western coast. They are led by Colga, King of Lochlann.'

'Colga? He has been threatening for many years to invade Ireland,' said Oisín gravely.

'The High King wants you to mobilise the Fianna and drive the Lochlannachs from our shores,' the messenger croaked, his voice rasping and his throat raw from the frantic ride.

Fionn jumped to his feet. 'Let us prepare for battle immediately!' He instructed Oisín to assemble the Fianna and told Oscar to arrange for food and drink to be given to the messenger. Then he hurried from the hall to don his armour and get his shield and weapons.

When the four battalions of the Fianna were drawn up in the fort, Fionn led them out to do battle. After half a day's march they saw the vast army of Lochlann bearing down on them from the crest of a hill. The invaders outnumbered them three to one and, at first, the fighting went against the Fianna. Then, just as they were about to give way, Fionn's ringing war-cry rallied them for one last extra effort and they held their ground. But they paid a high price for their bravery.

Oscar was furious when he saw so many of his comrades lying dead and wounded on the battlefield. Spying the standard of Colga, the Lochlann king, he carved his way towards him, his enemies falling before his great double-edged sword like corn under a scythe.

The king saw Oscar coming, and, with a contemptuous snarl, rushed to meet him. They fought each other savagely and mercilessly. Their shields bent and buckled under the flailing hail of sword blows. Their helmets were dented and their armour pierced with gaping holes. Blood flowed in red rivulets from their many wounds.

But Oscar gradually got the upper hand, and, seeing the king falter, he sheared his head from his shoulders with a massive blow of his sword.

The Lochlann army began to panic when word spread among them that their king was dead. They turned to flee back to their ships, but the Fianna pursued them relentlessly and cut them down, all but one. The survivor was Miodhach, the youngest son of Colga, and Fionn ordered that his life should be spared.

'I shall bring him up in my own household,' Fionn declared. He took the young prince back to the fort at the Hill of Allen, where he was given an honoured place.

❁   ❁   ❁

When Miodhach grew to manhood, he was trained for the gruelling trials a warrior had to undergo in order to be accepted into the Fianna. In one test he was hunted through the woods by other warriors. He had to run so lightly that no dry twig broke under his foot; if he stood on a thorn while fleeing from his pursuers, he had to pluck it out without stopping. If he was wounded or caught, or if his spear shook in his hand while he was defending himself, he would fail. Only if he succeeded in these, and many other trials of strength and courage, would he be accepted as a member of the Fianna.

Miodhach passed all the tests with flying colours. He joined the Fianna and Fionn made him one of his most trusted lieutenants. But Conán Mac Morna and many of the other leading Fianna warriors were not convinced of Miodhach's loyalty.

One day, when Miodhach was away on a hunting trip, they told Fionn of their suspicions.

'This young Lochlannach, Miodhach, has good cause to hate you and all of us in the Fianna,' said Conán. 'We killed his father and brothers before his very eyes.'

A murmur of agreement came from the others.

Fionn shook his head. 'I don't think there is any need for us to worry about Miodhach. He has grown up in my household, he has learned our ways, and I have never heard any word or seen any sign from him that he holds any hatred for us.'

'The loss of a father is not easily forgotten or forgiven. He has reason to hate us,' Conán insisted. 'I believe he is planning to have revenge. He says little but he learns all our secrets and our methods of waging war. I fear that the day may come when he will use this knowledge to try to destroy us.'

Again, there were murmurs of agreement from around the table. 'Very well then,' Fionn said with a shrug of his shoulders. 'I will heed your warnings. Has anyone any suggestion to make?'

'Send him far away from the fort,' advised Goll Mac Morna. 'Give him some land in a remote part of Ireland where he can have his own household if he wishes. Then he'll no longer be in a position to learn about our plans and secrets.'

'A sensible proposal,' Fionn agreed. 'I shall send him away, but I'll let him select the place where he wishes to live.'

Early next day Fionn summoned Miodhach and told him what had been arranged. The Lochlannach prince showed no anger or surprise, but thanked Fionn and chose for his dwelling a piece of land in the west which overlooked a sea inlet and a group of uninhabited islands.

As well as the land, Fionn gave him a house and cattle and a large amount of gold. Miodhach settled down in his new home. Over the years he grew wealthier and wealthier. But he never invited Fionn or any of his former Fianna comrades to visit him and enjoy his hospitality.

Instead, he plotted how best he could gain revenge on them for the deaths of his father and brothers. He knew he would need help from outside to defeat the Fianna and the many harbours and islands in his territory were ideal for a fleet of ships to anchor in safety and secrecy.

Finally, when he had gained enough wealth and power, he decided to put his plan into operation. He sent an invitation to kings and princes from Lochlann to come to Ireland with their armies to help destroy Fionn and the Fianna. In return, they would gain territory and slaves and a base in Ireland, which they had long desired. They all accepted his offer with enthusiasm, and together they set about preparing their deadly trap.

❀   ❀   ❀

Fionn and his companions were heading for a forest in the west that had a reputation for holding some of the finest and most ferocious wild boar in all of Ireland. It was a long and exhausting hunt and, when the chase was over, they had caught four fine beasts. As dusk was coming on they decided to set up camp for the night and pitched their tents on a hill near the edge of the forest, where they dug cooking-places and built a huge fire, ready for the evening meal.

They were sitting around the fire recalling the day's adventures when a tall warrior came striding up the hill towards them. He was dressed as if for battle, in a splendid coat of armour. On his left shoulder he carried a broad shield, and a great sword with a golden hilt hung from his belt. His helmet shone like burnished silver.

The warrior walked straight over to Fionn and greeted

him by name.

Fionn gave him a puzzled look. 'You have the advantage of me, stranger,' he said. 'I do not know you.'

'I recognise him,' said Conán. 'It is Miodhach, the Lochlannach.'

'I am no longer a Lochlannach,' Miodhach reminded him, 'I am a member of the Fianna, like yourself.'

'In name only,' Conán retorted, his voice harsh. 'In all the years you have lived in this part of the country you never invited Fionn or any of us to a feast, or offered us hospitality of any kind. That is not the way a true member of the Fianna should behave.'

'I am not to blame for that,' Miodhach protested. 'None of you needed an invitation to come to feast with a fellow member of the Fianna. That is one of our rules.'

A conciliatory smile lit up his face. 'However, now that you are here, I have arranged to hold a banquet tonight in your honour in one of my palaces. It is called the Palace of the Quicken Trees and you will find it near a ford to the east of this hill. I would be delighted to see you all there within an hour.'

He turned and strode away down the hill. Oisín stared questioningly at his father. 'Will you go?' he asked.

Fionn nodded. 'He has invited us and, as you know, I am bound by a *geas* – a solemn oath of honour – never to refuse an invitation to a feast.' He paused in thought and then turned to Conán. 'Would you like to go?'

Conán, the glutton of the Fianna, was torn between his love of fine food and his dislike of Miodhach.

'I still don't trust Miodhach,' he said. 'But it would be discourteous to refuse an invitation to a banquet,' he added, patting his ample stomach.

Fionn stared reflectively into the fire. 'I don't think we have anything to fear,' he said. 'However, just to be on the safe side, it might be advisable for only some of us to go to the feast and the rest to stay here.'

He placed his hand on Oisín's shoulder. 'You and Diarmaid Ó Duibhne and four others will remain in the camp. I will go with the rest to the Palace of the Quicken Trees. I will send back a messsenger to let you know that everything is alright.'

Fionn then set out with Conán Mac Morna, his brother Goll and ten other Fianna warriors.

❁   ❁   ❁

When Fionn's party drew near Miodhach's palace, they were astonished at its size and splendour. The building stood in a circle of quicken, or rowan, trees which were covered with clusters of gleaming red berries. On one side of the palace was a steep path leading down to a ford over a wide river. Although the side doors were closed, the main entrance was wide open. They approached the door and stopped. Fionn glanced around. There was no one to be seen and the palace had an eerie air about it.

'I find it strange that there is no one here to greet us. We are, after all, invited guests,' Fionn commented.

'Let me go in first and see what it's like,' Conán offered.

His stomach rumbled hungrily as he entered the palace. When he saw how magnificent the interior was, his eyes bulged with amazement. The walls were decorated in a variety of radiant colours. Soft couches, covered in gleaming silk, were placed in a circle around a huge smokeless fire. From the depths of the fire came a delightful fragrance which filled the room with its perfume. And, best of all in Conán's eyes, the golden tables which stretched the length of the room positively groaned under the weight of food. Roast pig, pheasant, venison and lamb were piled high on platters, surrounded by bowls of rare and delicious fruits and great flagons of wine and mead.

Conán rushed outside. 'Never in all my life have I seen a banqueting hall as splendid as this one!' he exclaimed. 'Come in and judge for yourselves.'

Fionn and the others entered the palace. They stood and stared in amazement at the richness and splendour of everything.

'No other king or chieftain in Ireland has a banqueting hall to compare with this!' declared Caoilte Mac Rónáin.

'But where is Miodhach?' asked Fionn uneasily. 'I do not understand why he is not here to welcome us.'

'We may as well sit down while we wait for him,' said Conán, licking his lips as he eyed the food.

They sat on the couches and waited. But there was still no sign of Miodhach. 'I am weak with hunger,' Conán complained. 'No one will mind if I help myself to a haunch of venison.'

But, just as his hand reached out to grasp his prize, all the fine food suddenly disappeared. Every table lay bare; goblets, wine, fruit and meats had vanished without trace. 'This is very strange,' growled a disappointed Conán.

'I see something even stranger,' Goll muttered. 'That fire, which was so clear and fragrant, is now foul and stinking and sending out clouds of black smoke.'

'There is something stranger than that,' Caoilte added. 'These walls, which were covered with radiant colours when we came in, are now nothing but rough quicken tree planks.'

'Look around,' said Conán. 'This hall, which had seven big doors leading from it, has now only one miserable door. And that is firmly closed.'

At this news, Fionn looked startled. 'This is very serious,' he said, 'I am under a *geas* never to stay in a quicken tree palace with only one door. It means great danger. Let us rise and break our way out through the walls.'

But as he and the others tried to get up, the couches under them vanished and they fell heavily to the ground, where they were stuck fast. Conán grabbed his spear and, planting it on the floor, tried to lever himself upright. But he remained fixed where he was. He tried again, leaning all his weight on the shaft of the spear. Beads of sweat ran down his forehead, his arms and shoulders ached with effort, and suddenly he lost his grip on his spear. He plunged headfirst to the floor, and when he tried to straighten up, found that he was fixed by the top of his head to the cold clay.

'Help me!' he cried out to his brother.

'How can I help? I can't move either,' Goll replied. 'Your suspicions were well-founded, Conán. There is no doubt that Miodhach is behind this treachery.'

He looked across at Fionn. 'Place your thumb in your mouth so that we may know the extent of the trouble we are in.' Fionn had acquired the power to foretell events in this way when he burnt his thumb on the salmon of knowledge, caught in the sacred waters of the River Boyne.

Fionn put his thumb in his mouth for several seconds, then withdrew it, looking very troubled. 'We are all in mortal danger. I can see no escape from Miodhach's terrible trap.'

'What does he intend to do to us?' Goll asked.

'He plans to kill us all,' Fionn replied. 'He has brought many Lochlannachs to this part of Ireland. They are commanded by Sinsear of the Battles, he who calls himself King of the World. With him are eighteen other kings and princes, and eighteen battalions of warriors. When they have disposed of us they will go after the High King and claim power over this land.'

Fionn glanced grimly at his comrades. 'There are three thousand men in each battalion,' he said ominously.

Goll shook his head. 'Then we are hopelessly outnumbered.'

'And while we are stuck to the ground like this, we can't even make a decent fight,' his brother added.

'Miodhach got the three kings of the Island of the Torrent to use their magical powers to cast a spell on us,' Fionn explained. 'They brought over clay from that enchanted island and placed it on the floor of this palace. It is that which keeps us stuck to the ground. The only way the spell can be broken is by spilling the blood of those same three kings on the clay.'

The others groaned loudly. It seemed hopeless. Fionn raised his hand. 'Lamentation will not help us,' he said. 'It is better that we should sound the Dord Fianna. Some of our comrades may hear us and come to our aid.' The Dord Fianna was a musical war-cry which the Fianna used in times of battle or danger.

So Fionn and his comrades began to sound the Dord Fianna in a last desperate attempt to escape death at the hands of their enemies.

✷ ✷ ✷

Oisín was getting worried. 'My father has been gone for hours. I wonder why he sent no messenger to us as he promised,' he said anxiously. 'Someone will have to go to the palace and find out what has happened.'

'I'll go,' volunteered Fionn's youngest son, Fiachna.

'And I will go with you,' said Inse Mac Suibhne, who was Fionn's foster-son.

They hurried away. As they approached the palace they heard the humming sound of the Dord Fianna.

'Things must be well with them if they are making music,' Inse observed.

21

Fiachna listened, then shook his head. 'When the Dord Fianna is sounded so slowly and sadly, it usually means danger.'

There was a lull in the Dord and Fionn heard the voices outside. 'Is that Fiachna,' he called out.

'Yes,' Fiachna replied. 'And Inse is here too.'

'Do not come any closer,' Fionn warned. 'Miodhach has betrayed us. This palace is full of spells and we are stuck to the ground by the sorcery of the three kings of the Island of the Torrent. Nothing can free us but the sprinkling of their blood on the clay beneath us.'

'What can we do to help?' Fiachna asked.

'Return to the camp at once and get Oisín and the others,' Fionn ordered. 'If you stay here you will both die under the swords of the Lochlannachs who will soon be on their way to the palace.'

But Fiachna and Inse refused to desert Fionn and the others. 'Well then, hurry to the ford nearby and prepare to defend it,' said Fionn. 'The Lochlannachs have to cross it in order to get to the palace.'

Fiachna and Inse ran back to the ford. 'One man can defend this,' Fiachna said. 'You stay here and guard it while I go and see what the Lochlannachs are up to.'

Inse drew his sword and took up position where the ford narrowed to a single passageway. He watched as Fiachna crossed to the far side and raced away.

❁   ❁   ❁

In the enchanted Quicken Tree Palace, Fionn and his

comrades were startled by the sound of loud mocking laughter outside the door. It opened suddenly and Miodhach appeared. He looked down on the helpless men. 'Don't go away!' he jeered. 'I have some other surprises in store for you. And don't lose your heads yet. It will be time to lose them later!' Still laughing, he slammed the door behind him and was gone before any of his hostages could respond.

Miodhach hurried off to his Island Palace where his Lochlannach friends were waiting. When he told them how Fionn and his companions had fallen into their trap they cheered jubilantly.

A prince among the King of the World's followers decided that he would go straightaway to cut off Fionn's head and bring it back to his king, thus gaining all the glory for himself.

The prince set off with a hundred of his warriors. As they arrived at the bank of the ford they saw Inse on the other side.

'What people do you belong to?' the prince demanded in a ringing voice.

'The people of Fionn Mac Cumhaill,' Inse responded.

'Then lead us to where Fionn is,' the prince ordered.

'Do not attempt to cross to this side of the ford,' Inse warned. 'Fionn sent me here to guard it and I will allow no one to pass alive.'

The prince turned to his followers. 'Kill him!' he ordered. Brandishing their weapons, the warriors rushed into the water. Because the ford was so narrow on Inse's side they could attack him only one at a time. With his mighty double-edged blade Inse cut each one down as they came against him. Soon, bodies of dead Lochlannachs were strewn all over the ford. The prince bellowed with rage and, weapon in hand, launched himself at Inse. The air rang with the clash of their weapons as they fought fiercely in the centre of the ford. But the prince was strong and fresh while Inse was tired and already wounded from combat. His knees buckled, and he fell to the ground. Before he could regain his feet, the prince's sword swept down and cut off his head. The prince raised the head triumphantly in the air and took it away to show the King of the World that he had slain Fionn Mac Cumhaill's foster-son.

Along the way he met Fiachna. 'Where have you come from?' he asked the prince.

'From the ford near the Palace of the Quicken Trees,' the prince said. 'I was on my way to kill Fionn Mac Cumhaill but this Fianna whelp was defending the ford and killed all my men.'

He bared his teeth in a wolfish grin and held up the head of Inse. 'See, I cut his head off. I am taking it to the King of the World, who will reward me well.'

Fiachna reached out and, taking the head, kissed it. 'Do you know to whom you have given this head?' he asked, his voice hoarse with grief.

'Are you not one of the King of the World's men?'

'I am not,' Fiachna said. 'And neither shall you be for much longer!'

He drew his sword and attacked the prince. The fight was short and savage. It ended when a powerful slanting blow from Fiachna's weapon felled the prince to the ground. Fiachna beheaded him and hurried with both heads back to the ford.

There he replaced Inse's head on his body and gave him an honourable burial. Then, carrying the prince's head, he raced back to the Palace of the Quicken Trees. From outside the door he shouted Fionn's name.

'Is that the voice of Fiachna?' Fionn called.

'It is indeed,' replied Fiachna. 'I have come with sad news. Our brave comrade, Inse, is dead. He defended the ford like a true hero, killing a hundred Lochlannachs, but he was slain by a prince of the King of the World's army. I have avenged Inse and cut off the prince's head.'

'My poor Inse,' said Fionn, mournfully. 'I loved him like my own son. He was a valiant warrior and his death does him honour, but it is a sad loss for all the Fianna.' Addressing Fiachna, he ordered: 'Return to the ford and defend it as bravely as Inse did. Our comrades may arrive in time to help us.'

Before Fiachna headed off he stuck the head of the prince on a spear and planted it in the ground outside the palace – a warning to their enemies that the Fianna were not easily defeated.

❈   ❈   ❈

In the Island Palace the rest of the Lochlannachs were waiting impatiently for Miodhach's battle orders. A prince called Ciorthainn was worried that his brother prince had not returned from the Enchanted Palace.

'I fear my brother is in trouble,' he said. 'I must go and find him.'

Taking four hundred warriors with him he set out for the Palace of the Quicken Trees. When they reached the ford they saw Fiachna, sword in hand, standing on the far side.

'Who are you?' Ciorthainn called out.

'I am Fiachna, youngest son of Fionn Mac Cumhaill,' Fiachna answered. 'And I warn you that if you try to cross this ford you will regret it.'

Ciorthainn's face turned red with rage. With a wild yell he led his men in a mad charge at the other side. Fiachna did not flinch but met them with his sword and shield. First he killed Ciorthainn and then cut down his men one by one, until the bodies of dead warriors lay in piles on either side of the ford. One warrior escaped the carnage and ran back frantically to the Island Palace.

Miodhach, who had been at a meeting with the King of the World, was furious when he heard what had happened. 'Those princes should never have gone to the ford without telling me! I know how the Fianna fight, and they had no hope of defeating them without that knowledge. I will go now and kill Fiachna. Then it will be the turn of Fionn and his companions to feel my revenge.'

His mouth twisted into a cruel smile. 'But it will not be quick. First I shall make them suffer. One of them, Conán Mac Morna, is the greatest glutton on earth. I will bring choice food and delicious drink to the palace to torment him with the sight and smell. Conán will lose his mind and while Fionn and the others are watching him suffer I will slowly kill them all.'

So, bringing the feast with him, he set off with five hundred of his best warriors. When they arrived at the ford, brave Fiachna was still guarding it.

'Is that my old comrade, Fiachna Mac Fhinn, I see?' Miodhach called across to him. 'You are very dear to me, Fiachna. During all the time I lived with the Fianna you were always kind to me and never lifted a hand in anger to any horse or hound or servant belonging to me.'

But Fiachna was not impressed by Miodhach's smooth talk. 'I had little to do with you in all the years you lived among the Fianna. But my father, Fionn, was very kind to you and you have repaid him with the foulest treachery and trickery.'

Miodhach almost choked with anger. In a voice no longer smooth and wheedling, he ordered Fiachna to leave the ford immediately. Fiachna laughed scornfully, 'I challenge you to make me.'

Miodhach ordered his warriors to attack. Swords drawn, they advanced on Fiachna. Like a wolf among sheep, Fiachna cut them down until he had killed them all. Mad at the slaughter of his men, Miodhach launched a ferocious attack on Fiachna with his razor-sharp broadsword. Wounded though he was from the previous battles, Fiachna responded with equal ferocity. The clash of their weapons echoed over the plain as they met in a frenzy of fury.

❀ ❀ ❀

In the Fianna camp Oisín was pacing up and down anxiously. 'Fiachna and Inse should have returned by now with news of Fionn and the others.'

'Perhaps they are enjoying the feast at the palace, too,' suggested Oscar.

Diarmaid Ó Duibhne shook his head doubtfully. 'They would not delay,' he said, 'knowing that we would be anxious for news. I had better go and see what is keeping them so long.'

'I'll go with you,' said his friend, Fatha Canann.

The two of them hurried off. As they approached the ford they heard the unmistakable sounds of battle. 'I hear Fiachna's war-shout,' said Diarmaid. 'He must be in combat with the Lochlannachs.

When they crested the hill overlooking the ford they saw below them a badly wounded Fiachna reeling under the savage blows of Miodhach's broadsword.

'Quick, Diarmaid!' cried Fatha. 'Save Fiachna.'

'By the time I reach them Miodhach will have killed him,' said Diarmaid. 'And if I throw my spear from here I may hit the wrong man.'

'Not you. You have never missed a target yet with it,' Fatha declared.

Diarmaid thrust his finger into the silken loop of his spear, drew back his arm, and with all his strength sent the deadly weapon screaming through the air. It was still travelling when it struck Miodhach, passed through his heart and hit the ground twenty feet away, where it stuck, quivering and vibrating like a living thing.

'Woe to him who is struck by that spear!' Miodhach cried out, 'for it belongs to Diarmaid Ó Duibhne.'

And, in his dying fury, he attacked Fiachna more fiercely than ever. Diarmaid started to rush across, shouting, 'Spare Fionn's son!'

'You have not spared me,' Miodhach snarled. 'So I shall make sure that Fionn never sees his son alive again!' He aimed a mighty blow at Fiachna and struck off his head.

'I will have your head in revenge!' Diarmaid shouted, and, with a sweep of his sword, he instantly beheaded Miodhach. He instructed Fatha to stand guard at the ford and set off for the Palace of the Quicken Trees. As he drew near he called out to Fionn.

'I recognise your voice, Diarmaid,' Fionn called back. 'Do not attempt to come in, this palace is full of magic spells. We have heard the sounds of a long and bitter fight at the ford. Tell me what happened.'

'Fionn,' said Diarmaid, his voice heavy with sorrow, 'your son Fiachna is dead. He killed many Lochlann warriors while defending the ford, but, when he was weak and wounded, he was struck down by the treacherous Miodhach Mac Colga. I have avenged his death and brought you the head of Miodhach.'

A great cry of lamentation went up inside the palace.

'My brave, loyal Fiachna,' Fionn mourned. 'He was a true son to me, and a gallant warrior who died as every member of the Fianna would wish to die, in battle for an honourable cause.'

Conán and the other Fianna in the palace raised their voices in praise and memory of Fiachna.

'Now, Diarmaid,' Fionn said, 'you have come to our assistance in many times of peril. But never before have I and my comrades here been in such danger as this. Through the treachery of Miodhach, we are stuck to the ground of this palace and can only be freed if the blood of the three kings of the Island of the Torrent is sprinkled on the clay. But, unless the ford is defended, the rest of the Lochlannachs will come here and kill us.'

'I and Fatha will keep them at bay,' declared Diarmaid. 'We will not let the sacrifices of Inse and Fiachna be in vain. I will return immediately to the ford.'

'Wait!' Conán cried out. 'I am tortured by hunger and thirst. Go and fetch as much food as you can find, as well as a drinking-horn full of wine.'

'Food? At a time like this? Am I to abandon my duty just to get food for Conán, the glutton?' Diarmaid demanded angrily.

'If I were a relation or close friend of yours you would soon give me what I ask,' Conán complained. 'But, just because we have had many disagreements in the past, you prefer to see me die of hunger and thirst.'

'Try to get some food for him, Diarmaid,' Fionn said. 'It will be a while before they come in search of Miodhach and for two hours now we have been tormented by Conán's wailing and moaning. I cannot stand it anymore. I need peace if I am to think of any way out of this situation. Find him something quickly; Fatha will watch the ford in the meantime.'

'Very well,' Diarmaid agreed, in a reluctant voice.

He returned to the ford and told Fatha of the trap Fionn and his companions were in. 'I promised to get Conán some food,' he concluded.

Fatha pointed to the food and drink that Miodhach had left on the far bank of the ford. 'That should provide a good feast for Conán,' he said.

Diarmaid shook his head. 'That food is tainted by the blood of our enemies. It would be poison to a Fianna warrior. I'll try somewhere else. Stay on guard until I return.'

Diarmaid set off for the Island Palace, where the rest of the Lochlannachs were holding a banquet in anticipation of Miodhach's triumphant return. He moved quietly to the door of the banqueting hall and peeped in. The kings and princes and their warriors were seated at long tables, enjoying the feast. Presiding over it all was Sinsear of the Battles, the self-styled King of the World. Beside him sat his son, Borba.

Diarmaid slipped into the hall and stood in a dark corner with his sword in his hand. When a servant carrying a drinking-horn of wine passed by, Diarmaid sheared his head from his body with one swift blow of his sword.

He caught the drinking-horn in his free hand as the man fell to the floor. Then he walked down the hall, snatched one of the dishes of food from Sinsear's table and hurried out through the door at the other end of the hall.

He ran back to the ford without spilling a drop of wine or a crumb of food. Fatha was lying asleep on the bank. At first Diarmaid was angry but then, realising that the young warrior was exhausted and that there was no immediate danger, he left him lying asleep and went on to the Palace of the Quicken Trees. 'Conán,' he called. 'I have brought the food you asked for. But how will I get it to you?'

'There is a hole in the wall opposite where I am lying,' replied Conán. 'Throw the food into my open mouth.'

Following Conán's directions, Diarmaid put his hand through the hole and threw the food across. But it struck Conán in the face and dribbled down his chin.

'I have a drinking-horn of wine for you, too,' Diarmaid said. 'How will I give it to you?'

'Climb up on the roof and make a hole above me,' Conán instructed. 'Then pour the wine into my mouth.'

Diarmaid climbed on to the roof of the palace and used the point of his spear to make a hole. He tipped the drinking-horn in and the wine poured out in a steady stream. However, it missed Conan's mouth entirely and splashed over his face and into his hair.

Conán spluttered angrily, complaining bitterly and loudly about Diarmaid's carelessness.

As he turned away from the palace to return to the ford, Diarmaid smiled to himself, the swears and curses of Conán accompanying him for much of his journey. 'That will teach him not to be always thinking of his belly,' he said aloud.

At the ford he found Fatha still sleeping soundly, but did not wake him, as all was quiet.

Meanwhile, word had reached the Lochlannachs at the Island Palace that Miodhach and all his warriors had been killed at the ford. The three kings of the Island of the Torrent almost choked with anger.

'We shall avenge their deaths!' one of them vowed, jumping to his feet. 'Let us go now and put an end to Fionn and his companions while they are still trapped.'

The others roared in agreement. The three kings set out with a thousand warriors and quickly reached the ford. There they saw Diarmaid standing guard on the far side.

'Who are you?' one of the kings shouted.

'I am Diarmaid Ó Duibhne of the Fianna. Fionn Mac Cumhaill has sent me here to guard the ford.'

'We are the three kings of the Island of the Torrent. We have heard of your great deeds and do not wish to harm you. So, if you will kindly leave the ford, we and our men will proceed peacefully on our way to the Palace of the Quicken Trees.'

Diarmaid shook his head determinedly. 'Fionn and his companions in the palace are under my protection. I will defend this ford as long as I have breath in my body.'

The kings immediately ordered their warriors to cross the ford and attack Diarmaid. As they came within range of his sword he killed them one by one. Wave after wave surged forward to take the place of their fallen comrades. But still Diarmaid did not give way.

The clash of weapons and the despairing cries of the wounded roused Fatha from his sleep. Livid with anger because Diarmaid had not woken him, he lunged at him with his fist. But Diarmaid shouted over his shoulder, 'Attack our enemies, not me!'

Drawing his sword, Fatha hurled himself into the fray. Lochlannachs fell in their dozens before his onslaught. Thinking that Diarmaid was weakening, the three kings attacked him fiercely. Diarmaid was forced to retreat to the bank of the river. Seeing him give ground, the kings shouted in triumph and followed him onto the bank. Slashing savagely with their spears and swords, they wounded him badly on his arms and shoulders.

Diarmaid fell back, blood streaming from his body and staining the earth around his feet. He knew that if the kings succeeded in killing him, Fionn and his comrades would soon suffer a similar fate. Drawing on his last reserves of strength and courage, he parried the kings' blows, and, with a great circular sweep of his sword, he killed all three of them, cutting off their heads with that single blow.

Fatha had by now slain the rest of the Lochlannachs. Carrying the kings' heads, Diarmaid and Fatha hurried back to the Enchanted Palace.

'I have killed the three kings of the Island of the Torrent,' Diarmaid cried out triumphantly, 'and I have brought their heads back.'

A great cheer came from inside the palace. 'Victory and blessings be always with you,' Fionn cried. 'Now, sprinkle some of their blood on the door.'

As soon as Diarmaid did so the door flew open. He and Fatha went inside and saw how Fionn and the others were stuck to the ground.

Beginning with Fionn, they sprinkled blood on the clay beneath him and his companions. The spell was broken at once. Fionn and the warriors sprang jubilantly to their feet, stretching their aching muscles. Only Conán remained where he was, glued fast to the ground by the top of his head where the blood had not reached.

'Are you going to leave me here like this?' he growled, glaring at Diarmaid.

'There is no more blood left,' Diarmaid explained, holding up the drained heads. 'I will try to pull you free.'

He caught Conán by the arms and, with a mighty heave, hauled him to his feet. There was a terrible ripping sound as Conán's body broke free, leaving the skin and hair from the top of his head stuck to the ground. Conán was about to cry out in anger and pain when a cold glance from Fionn told him that, for once, he had better hold his peace.

'We are not yet out of danger,' Fionn warned them all. 'We are weak from the effect of the spells and are in no state to fight. But we will regain our power at sunrise.' He turned to Diarmaid. 'In the meantime you and Fatha will have to continue to guard the ford.'

And so Diarmaid and Fatha set off to stand watch on the ford once more.

❈　　❈　　❈

When word reached Sinsear, King of the World, and his people that the kings of the Island of the Torrent and their followers had been killed, Borba, son of the King of the World, declared that he would go and bring Fionn's head back to his father.

Off he went, with hundreds of heavily armed warriors. They arrived at the ford with a great clanking of armour and weapons. Immediately they saw Diarmaid and Fatha they rushed across to attack them.

'We are greatly outnumbered,' Diarmaid said to Fatha. 'But if we can just hold off until sunrise, Fionn and the others will come to our aid.'

The bloody combat began. Hard-pressed as they were, Fatha and Diarmaid yielded not an inch but stood shoulder to shoulder against their foes.

When at last the sun rose over the Palace of the Quicken Trees, Fionn, Conán, Goll and the others felt the strength flowing back into their bodies. They charged to the ford at full speed to help their embattled comrades.

Although by now exhausted and wounded, Diarmaid and Fatha were still holding the ford. Despite their great advantage in numbers, the Lochlannachs were only able to attack two at a time because of the narrow space where Diarmaid and Fatha had taken up their positions. This enabled one of them to deal with the Lochlannachs advancing on the left while his comrade dealt with those advancing on the right.

Suddenly they heard a loud shout behind them and Fionn and his companions came racing down the hill to help them. They launched themselves at the Lochlannachs and quickly drove them back.

❋   ❋   ❋

Oisín still had no word of his father, nor of any of the Fianna who had gone after him. He decided to see for himself what was happening. When he and his men arrived at the ford they immediately joined in the fight.

Goll Mac Morna found himself facing Borba, the King of the World's son. They fought each other in long and deadly combat. Goll finally got the upper hand and, with a sweep of his sword, sent the mortally wounded Borba flying into the swirling waters.

The remaining Lochlann warriors turned and fled. The Fianna pursued and killed most of them, but two managed to escape back to the Island Palace. Rushing into the hall, they told the King of the World how his son had been killed and his army defeated.

The king swore to have swift vengeance on Fionn and the Fianna. Summoning all his remaining warriors, his princes and chieftains, he led his vast army to the ford. Fionn and the others were still drawing their breath from the battle just ended when the enormous horde swept down on them.

But the main group of Fianna at the fort on the Hill of Allen had heard of the danger that Fionn and his comrades were in and were already making a forced march towards the ford.

The nimble-footed Clann Baoiscne led the first

battalion. The stalwart Clann Morna led the second. The strong-armed Clann Mic an Smoil led the third, and the fearless Clann Neamhain led the fourth. As they marched along, their burnished weapons glittered in the sun.

They arrived at the ford just in time to help their hard-pressed comrades. Before the Lochlannachs could turn to face them, a hail of spears whistled through the air and killed many of them on the spot.

The Fianna then drew their mighty swords and waded into the widest part of the ford to meet the enemy in close combat. So closely did they fight that at times it was hard to distinguish between friend and foe. But at last the rapidly thinning numbers of the enemy began to fall back and scatter in panic.

Oscar, Fionn's grandson, spied the standard of the King of the World where he stood in a protective circle of his best warriors. Like an enraged lion, Oscar cleaved his way through their ranks until he came face to face with the king.

The king swung his sword and the blade bit deeply into Oscar's shoulder. Ignoring the searing pain, Oscar responded with a blow of his sword that sliced off the king's right ear.

Bellowing with rage, the king flailed savagely at Oscar. The young Fianna warrior began to retreat before the ferocity of the attack. But, hearing a shout of encourage-ment from Fionn, he fought back and knocked the king's shield from his grasp. Then, with a swift blow, he swept the king's head from his body.

A great shout of triumph erupted from the ranks of the Fianna and what was left of the Lochlann army turned and took to their heels. The Fianna pursued them and killed many of them. Those who managed to get back to their ships sailed home as fast as they could.

And never again did any of them dare to venture near the shores of Ireland.

As for Conán Mac Morna, the hair which he had lost in the Enchanted Palace never grew again, and from that time on he was known among the Fianna as Conán Maol or Conán the Bald – a blow to his great pride and a fitting punishment for his selfishness and gluttony.

Che quest for the Giolla Oeacair

Following their defeat by the Fianna, the Tuatha Dé Danann were always on the watch for a chance to work some mischief on their old enemies. The hunting season was a favourite time for the Tuatha to brew up some of their magical tricks and catch the Fianna off-guard.

This thought disturbed the contentment of Fionn Mac Cumhaill as he and a group of the Fianna followed their hounds on a bright midsummer's day hunt.

'Who will go to the highest point on that hill and keep a watch out for any stranger that may come this way?' he asked. 'It is at a time like this, when we are all relaxed, that the Tuatha Dé Danann are most likely to play a trick on us.'

'I will,' offered the young warrior Fionn Mac Breasail.

Clutching his weapons firmly, he went to the hilltop and took up position. From there he had a clear view over all the surrounding countryside.

As he turned to look eastwards, his gaze fastened on a giant of a man approaching the hill and pulling a large, shambling horse behind him. It seemed to Mac Breasail that this man was the ugliest person he had ever seen.

His huge body was ill-shaped and bloated. His legs were crooked. His mouth was twisted, and long pointed teeth projected from it at all angles. His eyes were like black holes in the skull of a corpse. Although the man carried a full array of weapons, they were rusted and neglected. A battered and broken old shield was slung from his right shoulder. In one hand he held a large iron club which he dragged along after him, so that it left a deep trench in the ground.

The horse trailing behind was an even sorrier sight. Dirty, shaggy hair covered its long, spiny back and the ribs were sticking out through its sides. Its legs and feet were crooked and splayed and a head that seemed too large for his body dangled awkwardly from a scrawny neck.

The animal walked very slowly and very reluctantly behind its master. Whenever it tried to stop to graze, the man clattered its ribs with his club.

Fionn Mac Breasail was not a coward, but when he saw the grotesque figures of the man and horse draw near, he thought he was looking at a demon sent from the Otherworld. He turned, and half-ran, half-tumbled

41

back down the hill to where Fionn and his companions were resting.

Fionn Mac Cumhaill glanced up from the game of chess he was playing. 'What is the matter?' he asked curtly. Mac Breasail did not reply but pointed a trembling finger towards the hilltop. Fionn and his comrades stared in amazement at the weird-looking man and the even weirder horse coming towards them. The man stopped beside Fionn and saluted him.

Fionn looked at him questioningly. 'Who are you and where do you come from?' he asked.

'I am a Fomhórach from the northern land of Lochlann,' said the man, in a gravelly voice that seemed to come from the very depths of his body. 'I travel around from one country to another, serving great chieftains like yourself, in return for what I consider to be a fair wage. I have come here today to ask you to take me into your service.'

The Fomhórach bowed. 'I am known, by the way, as An Giolla Deacair.'

'An Giolla Deacair? The Troublesome Slave? Surely,' said Fionn, 'that is the name given to a lazy, worthless fellow?'

'I will be honest with you,' the Giolla Deacair replied. 'There is no servant in all the world lazier than I am. As well as that, I am a very difficult person to deal with. Even if my master should be very kind to me, I will give him no thanks or credit for it.'

Fionn smiled. 'You are certainly honest, anyway, even

if you are unpleasant and hard to deal with. But I have never refused service and wages to anyone who asked me. I shall not refuse you either.'

So, he agreed to take the Giolla Deacair into his service. Then he resumed his game of chess. The Giolla Deacair went over to talk to Conán Maol, the fattest, greediest and most ill-tempered man in the Fianna.

'Who gets the best pay in the Fianna?' he asked, 'a foot-soldier or a horse-soldier?'

'A horse-soldier,' replied Conán.

'Then I will join the horse-soldiers. As you see, I have a fine horse of my own.'

'That bag of bones!' Conán guffawed. 'Call that a horse? It can hardly stand on its feet.'

'It is an excellent steed,' the Giolla Deacair declared, indignantly. 'I would not trust anyone to look after it except myself.'

Fionn and his companions burst into raucous laughter. Ignoring their hoots of derision, the Giolla led his horse to the field where the Fianna's horses were grazing on the rich grass.

But, instead of joining them in peaceful grazing, the strange horse began to wreak havoc among the other animals. It kicked out viciously in all directions. It crippled some horses and bit others with its long crooked teeth.

The Giolla's horse then left that field and headed for the next field where Conán's horses were grazing separately.

With a fierce oath, Conán yelled to the Giolla Deacair

to take his horse away before it did any further damage.

'If you do not stop that mad brute of yours, I will knock it senseless!' he threatened.

'The only way to stop it is to put the halter on it,' the Giolla said. 'But then it would be unable to graze and would grow weak and hungry.'

'It can die for all I care,' Conán growled. 'Put the halter on it.'

'Do it yourself,' the Giolla said. 'I can't be bothered.'

Conán grabbed the halter and ran to the horse. He flung the halter over the animal's head and tried to lead it away. The animal stopped immediately. Its body and legs froze and, despite his great strength, Conán could not make it budge an inch.

He tugged and strained at the halter, but still the horse refused to move. The others all mocked Conán.

'Poor Conán,' said his brother, Goll. 'Look how weak he is. He musn't be getting enough to eat!'

Feargus Finnbéal, the poet, advised him to mount the horse and gallop it over the rough countryside so as to break its spirit and make it obedient.

Conán leaped up on the horse's back and tried to make it move. The horse remained motionless.

'It is used to carrying the Giolla Deacair, who is heavier than you,' said Feargus. 'It will not budge until it has a similar weight on its back.'

Conán stared appealingly at his comrades. 'You heard what Feargus said. Which of you will get up on the horse's back with me?'

'I will!' shouted Cóil Cróga, leaping up on the horse behind Conán. Still the animal refused to move. Others piled on. Soon there were fourteen of the Fianna sitting behind Conán on the horse's very long, very uncomfortable back. They pounded the animal with their fists and dug their heels into its sides, but still it refused to shift.

The Giolla Deacair went over to Fionn. 'Your men are ill-treating my horse,' he protested. 'I am sorry now that I agreed to enter your service. I will not stay here another second!' He turned and set off slowly. When the horse saw him leaving, it began to move after him, with the fifteen Fianna warriors still on its back.

The Giolla Deacair suddenly increased the length of his strides and headed off quickly in a southwesterly direction. The horse broke into a canter and then a gallop as it followed its master. The men on its back tried to jump off, but found to their dismay that they were welded to the horse like a sword to its hilt. The rest of the Fianna had a good laugh at their predicament. Conán threw a desperate glance back at the receding figures of Fionn and the others.

'Shame on you all!' he shouted. 'Are you willing to stand by and let your comrades be borne away by this ugly animal?'

Fionn signalled to the others to join him in following the horse and the Giolla. They set off in pursuit, but no matter how fast they went, the Giolla and his horse went faster, travelling like the wind over mountains, valleys and rivers.

Soon the Giolla disappeared from sight. Then, just as the Fianna thought that the horse had also eluded them, they saw it standing on a strand by the very edge of the sea.

The warrior who was leading the chase managed to get a grip on the horse's tail. He held on tightly, hoping to delay the animal until the others arrived to help him. But the horse shot into the waves, dragging the man after him. When he tried to let go, he found that both his hands were stuck firmly to the animal's tail.

The horse continued on its journey through the sea. The waves did not touch it nor the fifteen Fianna on its back, nor the unfortunate man clinging to its tail. Instead, the water parted before the animal, so that it travelled on a path of dry ground.

Fionn and his companions stood, crestfallen, on the strand, watching their comrades disappear from view and wondering would they ever see them again. Fionn turned sadly to Feargus.

'Is there nothing more we can do to help them?' he asked.

Feargus gazed thoughtfully out to sea. 'We should find a ship and search for them.'

Fionn and the others agreed. On their way to their camp they met two brothers, Fearadach and Foltlár, and told them about the Giolla's trick and how they were looking for a ship to follow him.

'I am a skilled builder of ships,' Fearadach replied.

'And I am an expert tracker,' Foltlár added, 'on sea as well as on land. We would like to help you.'

'We need a shipbuilder,' Fionn said. 'And, although we have the most skilled trackers on land, we have none who can also track on sea. We would welcome your help.'

When the ship was ready, Fionn selected his grandson, Oscar, as well as Diarmaid Ó Duibhne, Conán and his brother Goll, and Fearadach, Foltlár and ten others to accompany him on the quest for the Giolla Deacair. He instructed his son, Oisín, to remain in Ireland in charge of the rest of the Fianna while he was away. Then he and the others set sail in the direction the horse had taken.

❀　❀　❀

After many days' voyaging they arrived at the base of a cliff which soared so high into the sky that the peak almost touched the clouds.

'This is where the track of the Giolla Deacair runs out,' Foltlár said. 'He and his horse, and the men stuck on its back, must have travelled on over that cliff.'

Fionn stared up at the rock and shook his head gloomily. 'I can't see a way to the top of that,' he declared. There was a murmur of agreement from his companions. Then Feargus spoke up.

'There is one among us who could do it,' he said, 'if he has not lost his daring and courage.' He stared meaningfully at Diarmaid.

Diarmaid craned his neck to look up at the towering cliff. 'It is a very hard challenge you place before me,' he said. 'But, for the sake of our comrades, I will do my best to climb the cliff.'

He buckled on his sword, harnessed his spear to his back with one of the ship's ropes and began to climb. It was slow, dangerous progress as he searched for footholds in the cracks in the rock. Halfway up, a shrieking gull flew out of her nest, right in front of his face. Startled, Diarmaid jerked back; his feet slipped from under him and he was left dangling by his fingertips. His friends gasped, as, for what seemed like an eternity, he hung from the vertical drop. Then his desperate feet found a niche and he hauled himself upwards again.

At last he reached the summit, and, tying the rope securely to a big boulder, he lowered it down to his comrades. 'I will go ahead,' he shouted, his voice faint and echoing. 'You can follow my tracks.'

Then he set out across the plain that stretched before him. After travelling for a short while he came to a well full of clear spring water. He placed a mark on the side of the well for his comrades to see. On a nearby ledge lay a richly ornamented drinking-horn. Taking the horn, he filled it from the well and had a long refreshing drink.

Suddenly he heard a furious bellow behind him. Swirling around, he saw a tall, fully armed warrior striding towards him.

'Who gave you permission to drink from my well with my drinking-horn?' he shouted. 'I will have satisfaction from you!'

Drawing his sword, the warrior rushed at Diarmaid. The Fianna warrior immediately drew his own sword to defend himself.

They fought for hours. Wide cracks appeared on their shields as they slashed at each other with their great weapons. Then Diarmaid's opponent began to tire. He edged away and was about to jump into the well when Diarmaid managed to get a tight grip on him.

'You will not escape that easily!' he said. The warrior struggled to free himself. They swayed on the edge of the well and then both toppled in.

Still grasping each other, they sank deeper and deeper in the water. Just as Diarmaid began to think that there was no bottom to this well, and that he was condemned to a watery grave, his feet touched solid ground. The well-water surged up and away and, to his amazement, Diarmaid found himself standing in beautiful countryside, with fertile valleys, green hills and leafy woods. He let go his grip on the other man, who immediately disappeared.

In the distance Diarmaid saw a city with a large, imposing palace. He went towards it. When he reached the green in front of the palace he saw that it was occupied by a group of warriors, practising armed combat. Then he spied his enemy from the well, running towards the palace entrance.

Diarmaid tried to follow him but his way was blocked by the warriors. They menaced him with their weapons, but Diarmaid drew his sword and, with a loud battle-cry, cleaved his way through the group.

Those who survived his onslaught ran into the palace and barricaded themselves inside. Tired and wounded, Diarmaid lay down behind a hedge to snatch some sleep.

He was awakened by a tap on his shoulder. Looking up, he saw a young warrior with sword in hand.

Instinctively, Diarmaid grabbed his own sword and jumped to his feet. But the stranger gave him a friendly smile and said, 'I am the Knight of Valour. I mean you no harm. My only wish is to help you. Come with me to a safe place where you can rest and recover your strength.'

Diarmaid followed his new friend to a large house some miles away. The man brought him into a banqueting hall where a magnificent feast was in progress. Diarmaid was introduced to all the lords and ladies in the hall and sat down with them to enjoy the feast.

When he had eaten and drunk his fill, Diarmaid thanked his host for his hospitality.

'Tell me the name of this country,' he said. 'I would also like to know the name of the warrior who escaped from me at the palace.'

'This country is called Tír Faoi Thoinn, the land beneath the sea,' his host replied. 'The warrior is known as the Knight of the Well. He is my brother and is now king of this country. But, although we are brothers, we are sworn enemies. He unfairly deprived me of most of the land and inheritance our late father, the old king, left to me.'

He paused and put his hand on Diarmaid's shoulder. 'I saw how you dealt with my brothers' warriors; I would be glad of your help to win back what is rightfully mine.'

'I will help willingly,' Diarmaid replied, 'if, in return, you will assist me in finding my friends who have been kidnapped by a creature known as the Giolla Deacair. We tracked them as far as the cliff that borders the land by the well, but I have seen no sign of them since.'

'I have one hundred and fifty warriors here,' the prince replied. If you lead them into battle against my evil brother, they will be at your disposal to find your comrades.'

'Fear not,' Diarmaid assured him, 'I will not rest until you have regained what is yours by right.'

⊗   ⊗   ⊗

Fionn and the others had succeeded in climbing the hill and were following Diarmaid's tracks. When they reached the well they saw the mark he had left. Foltlár inspected the ground.

'There is no sign of Diarmaid's tracks continuing on here,' he said. 'There is only one way he could have gone – down through the well.'

'Then we shall have to go that way too,' Fionn declared. He jumped into the well, followed by the others. They sank to the bottom and, just as Diarmaid had, they emerged into the beautiful Tír Faoi Thoinn.

Foltlár picked up Diarmaid's tracks again and they followed them over the plain. They had just stopped for a brief rest when they saw a large group of armed warriors approaching them.

'Look!' exclaimed Goll Mac Morna. 'That is Diarmaid Ó Duibhne at their head.'

Fionn and the others shouted joyfully and ran forward

to greet Diarmaid. He told them of his adventures since he had left them at the cliff.

'These are the men of the Knight of Valour,' he said, gesturing at the group behind him. 'We are coming from a great battle in which we defeated the army of the evil king of this land. I myself killed the king in single combat.'

He beckoned the knight forward. 'And this is my friend, the Knight of Valour, who is now King of Tír Faoi Thoinn. He has promised to help us find Conán and the others.'

The new king greeted Fionn and his companions. 'Diarmaid told me of your quest,' he said. 'I have found out that the Giolla Deacair is really Abhartha, a Tuatha Dé Danann magician. He is holding your people at an enchanted fort on the far side of those hills.'

'We shall go at once and free them,' Fionn said.

'I and my men would be glad to help you,' offered the king.

Fionn thanked him and assured him that he and his companions could deal with Abhartha themselves. Then, with Diarmaid accompanying them, they set off again in quest of the so-called Giolla Deacair.

They made their way across the hills and came within sight of the Giolla's fort. They stopped to formulate a plan. Goll Mac Morna suggested launching a surprise attack on Abhartha and his men.

Fionn disagreed. 'I think it would be best if we sent a messenger to Abhartha asking him to free our comrades. If we were to attack him suddenly he might kill them in revenge.' His face grew grim. 'But, if he refuses to comply, we shall have no mercy on him or his people.'

The wise and silver-tongued Feargus Finnbéal was sent as an emissary to the Giolla. He was surprised to see his kidnapped comrades playing games on the green in front of the fort. They rushed to greet him.

Hearing the commotion, Abhartha emerged from the fort. 'I am an ambassador from Fionn Mac Cumhaill,' Feargus told him. 'He and his men are near your fort. He has sent me to ask you to free our comrades. Otherwise, the Fianna will wage terrible war on you and your people.'

'As you can see, I have treated your comrades with kindness,' Abhartha said. 'Neither I, nor any of my people, wish to meet the Fianna in war again. We know that we have no hope of defeating them in battle. So, I will gladly set your comrades free and pay whatever fine Fionn decides on as a penalty for the trick I played. Go back to Fionn and tell him that. Tell him also that he and his companions are welcome to join me here in a feast to celebrate the renewed peace between us.'

Feargus returned to Fionn and told him what Abhartha had said. They all went to the fort, where Abhartha gave them a hundred thousand welcomes. He led them into his banqueting hall, where a magnificent feast was laid out on the tables. When they had finished eating, Abhartha turned to Fionn and said, 'Now, name the penalty you wish to impose on me.'

Fionn pondered for a while. 'In fairness, I think that one of the men you kidnapped should decide on the penalty. I will abide by his suggestion.'

Conán Maol immediately jumped to his feet. 'I was the first to suffer!' he said. 'Let me choose the penalty.'

'Very well then,' Abhartha said. 'Name the penalty and I will carry it out.'

'My decision is as follows,' Conán declared. 'Fifteen of your men are to go on the back of that creature you call a horse. You are to hold on to its tail. Then you are all to go back to Ireland, in the same way that your horse carried us here.'

Abhartha agreed to this. Fionn and his companions returned to the cliff, lowered themselves on the rope to the deck of the ship and sailed back to Ireland. They were on exactly the same hill where the Giolla had first appeared when they spied the bony horse, bumping and jolting towards them with fifteen Tuatha Dé Danann clinging desperately to its back and the Giolla Deacair hanging on to its tail.

Fionn and the others burst out laughing when they saw how dishevelled and uncomfortable the group looked.

'That was indeed a very good penalty, Conán!' Fionn exclaimed.

They were continuing to enjoy the spectacle when the Giolla Deacair suddenly pointed to the top of the hill. Fionn and his companions swung around to see what had caught the Giolla's attention. There was nothing there.

When they turned back, the Giolla Deacair, his men

and the horse had all disappeared. And from that day on neither Fionn nor any of the Fianna ever saw them again.

But, for years afterwards, the story of the quest for the Giolla Deacair was told and re-told by the fires at night, serving as a reminder to the Fianna that they should always be on their guard for the tricks of the Tuatha Dé Danann.

OISÍN AND NIAMH
CINN ÓIR

It was an ideal morning for hunting. The trees and hedges were fragrant with blossoms and no cloud smudged the bright sapphire of the sky. The woods were full of deer. When they heard the baying of Sceolaing and Bran, Fionn's hounds, they dashed from cover and went bounding over the plain leading down to the waters of Loch Léin.

Fionn, his son, Oisín, and their Fianna comrades were so engrossed in the chase that at first they did not notice the rider on the pure white horse approaching swiftly from the west. But the ever-alert Caoilte Mac Rónáin spotted the steed as he paused to take an arrow from his deerskin quiver.

'Look!' he shouted. 'Someone is coming!'

Fionn and the others reached for their swords. The Fianna had defeated the Tuatha Dé Danann many years before, but the Tuatha occasionally sent people from their underground home to try to kill Fionn or Oisín or Oscar in revenge.

Fionn's eyes narrowed as the rider came nearer. Then they opened wide in surprise.

'That is not one of the Tuatha Dé Danann,' he exclaimed. 'It is a beautiful young maiden.'

The girl on the white steed approached and stopped. She wore a silken robe covered in glittering stars that shone like the brightest of diamonds. Her hair flowed over her shoulders and down to her waist like a river of molten gold. Her eyes were large and green. On her head she wore a crown encrusted with precious stones.

Oisín was entranced by this vision. 'I have never seen anyone lovelier,' he murmured.

The horse was an elegant pure-bred stallion, his hindquarters covered in a satin cloth and his shoes made of finest gold. The girl sat confidently on the horse's back and held the bridle with a small but strong hand.

'Who are you, lovely lady?' Fionn enquired. 'And where do you come from?'

'Noble leader of the Fianna,' she answered in a sweet voice, 'I come from a country far over the western sea, called Tír na nÓg, Land of Eternal Youth. My name is Niamh Cinn Óir and I am the daughter of the king.'

'Tell me, Niamh of the Golden Hair, what has brought you here? Has your husband abandoned you, or has some other trouble befallen you, that you seek the help of the Fianna?'

Niamh smiled and shook her head. 'I have never been married or betrothed to any man. But, in a dream, I saw the man I wish to marry. He lives here in Ireland.'

'What is the name of this fortunate man?' Fionn asked.

'He is called Oisín, and he stands there beside you.'

'Oisín, my son?'

'Yes, your son,' Niamh declared. 'Even in far-off Tír na nÓg we have heard the stories of his bravery, his courtesy, his honour and his gentleness. Many princes have sought my hand in marriage, but the only man I can ever love is Oisín.'

Fionn glanced at Oisín and asked, 'What is your response to this lady?'

Oisín did not reply but moved closer to the white steed. He looked at the lovely maiden with her golden hair and smiling eyes. She leaned forward to speak to him. 'As well as bringing you my love, Oisín, I also bring you the opportunity to enjoy eternal youth,' she said softly.

'You do?' Oisín said, entranced by her words and her beauty.

'If you come with me on my white steed to Tír na nÓg, the Land of Eternal Youth, you will always stay as young and as strong as you are today; you will never grow old or feeble, you will never suffer pain or disability. Besides all this, Tír na nÓg is a delightful country, full of milk and honey and trees that bear fruit all the year round.

She paused and pressed his hand. 'As my husband, you will be honoured; you will be given gold and silver and precious jewels, a hundred swift horses and a hundred keen-scenting hounds. You will also have great herds of the finest cattle and flocks of golden-fleeced sheep. You will receive a coat of armour that cannot be pierced and a sword that will kill anyone you meet in battle. And my father, the king of Tír na nÓg, will present you with a golden crown which will protect you from all harm and danger.'

Oisín's eyes widened in wonder. 'To possess all these, and to have everlasting youth, is beyond anything I have ever dreamed of,' he muttered.

'And to have me as your wife,' she reminded him, smiling.

'Of course,' Oisín said, now completely enchanted by Niamh's beauty and charm. 'That would make me the happiest man alive.'

'Are you ready to come with me now?' she asked.

Oisín turned to Fionn. 'Father, I have made up my mind. I have decided that I wish to go with Niamh to the Land of Youth. But I would like to have your blessing before I go.'

Fionn shook his head sadly. Laying his hand on Oisín's shoulder he said, 'I would not want to stand in the way of your happiness, my son. And, in truth, I have never seen a maiden as worthy of you as Niamh of the Golden Hair. But I would be very sad to lose you. And something about all this troubles me. I feel in my heart that if you leave now you will never come back to Ireland and I will never see you again.'

'No, father, I shall return to Ireland,' Oisín promised.

Even as he said these words, Oisín felt a strange sense of foreboding. He loved his father and his adventurous life with the Fianna. But his love for Niamh was stronger than any emotion he had experienced before. And there was the exciting challenge of a new life in a strange land where he would never grow old. Of course, he could never forget Fionn and the Fianna. Or could he?

The soft voice of Niamh quelled his doubts. 'Come,' she said, her emerald eyes holding his in a loving gaze.

Oisín turned to his father and comrades and bade them farewell. He mounted the white steed behind Niamh. She signalled to the horse and he galloped away swiftly to the west. Before they disappeared over the horizon, Oisín turned and saw Fionn, one hand raised in farewell, the other shading his eyes for one last glimpse of his beloved son.

❈   ❈   ❈

When they arrived at a strand on the edge of Ireland, the horse zoomed out over the sea. He sped like the wind over the top of the ocean, the waves leaping high and furiously, but never succeeding in touching the golden-shod hooves. Soon, Niamh and Oisín had left the land of Ireland far behind.

As they passed over the sea strange sights appeared: a small deer crossed in front of them, bounding along from the top of one wave to the crest of another. In close pursuit of it came came a white hound with red ears.

Both animals raced away over the waves and vanished from sight. Then Oisín saw a lovely young girl on a brown horse. She was carrying a golden apple in her hand. As she travelled over the waves, a young warrior on a white horse came after her, holding a gold-hilted sword in his hand.

'What do these strange sights mean?' Oisín asked Niamh.

'They are signs that we have left the ordinary world and entered another world of magic and enchantment where things are not always what they seem. But these wonders are nothing compared to those you will see when we arrive in Tír na nÓg.'

They glided swiftly along until they spied beneath them a large island rising out of the sea. A splendid white palace stood in the centre, with a high tower at each of its four corners.

'Who does that palace belong to?' Oisín enquired.

'It is the palace of the king of giants. He is known as Fomor of the Blows. His future queen is the daughter of the king of the Land of Life. Fomor took her by force from her own country and keeps her prisoner on the island.'

'Why are they not married?'

'She has put him under a *geas*, a sworn oath, never to marry her until she finds a champion to fight him in single combat. She knows that no one is likely to take on the task and so she has been able to put off the marriage, which she dreads. But it is very sad for her because she is destined to remain Fomor's prisoner forever.'

Oisín drew a deep breath. 'I feel sorry for the princess. If you have no objection, I will go to the palace and kill the giant so that she will have her freedom.'

'It is what I would expect a hero like you to do,' Niamh smiled. She signalled to the steed and he landed close to the palace.

The young princess came out and welcomed them. She led them into the palace and, seating them on golden chairs, she gave them choice foods and drinking-horns filled with delicious mead made from the finest honey.

When they had finished eating and drinking the princess told them her sad story. With tears in her eyes she said, 'I will never see my mother and my country again as long as the cruel giant is alive!'

Oisín sprang to his feet and promised to be her champion. Just then, a huge ugly giant thumped into the palace. He carried a large iron club in his hand. Pointing it menacingly at Oisín, he challenged him to combat.

Oisín followed Fomor out to the green in front of the palace. Niamh and the princess watched anxiously from a window.

Although Oisín had fought many times in single combat, this fight was the hardest of his life. The duel lasted for three days and three nights, without pause for food or drink or sleep.

Time and again the giant's iron club slipped through Oisín's guard and thudded with bone-shattering force into his body. Whenever Oisín tried to wound Fomor, the monster evaded his sword with astonishing agility for a man of his immense bulk.

Niamh and the princess grew more anxious as they saw Oisín beginning to give way in the fight. If the giant emerged as victor, Niamh would lose her beloved Oisín and she trembled to think of what her fate might be then.

Oisín too was thinking of the awful consequences of his defeat. He gritted his teeth, summoning all of his strength for one final desperate effort.

His sudden onslaught sent the giant reeling back. Fomor stumbled and slipped to the ground. Oisín brought his great sword down on the giant's neck and the blade went clean through. Fomor's head rolled away over the grass.

Niamh and the princess shouted with joy. They helped Oisín into the palace where they healed his wounds with magical herbs and ointments. Soon he felt his strength beginning to return.

After they had rested, Niamh said that it was time for them to resume their journey to Tír na nÓg. They bid farewell to the princess and mounted the white steed. At a word from Niamh, the horse galloped off towards the strand and launched himself out over the waves.

❀   ❀   ❀

Once again they glided over the vast blue-green sea. The sky darkened suddenly and the sun retreated behind a veil of clouds. A violent storm broke around them. Jagged flashes of lightning lit up the sea. The wind howled and blew in fierce gusts. The waves below them were whipped into a frenzy. But the white steed moved swiftly over it all, unaffected by the force of the raging elements.

The storm finally died away and the sun shone brightly again. Looking down, Oisín saw that they were approaching another country. It had wide green plains, purple hills and shimmering lakes and waterfalls.

In the centre stood a splendid palace encrusted with gold and gems of various colours. As the sun reflected off the jewelled roofs it sent multicoloured beams into the air, surrounding the island with a hundred rainbows.

Oisín had never seen anywhere as wonderful-looking. 'What country is that?' he asked.

'That is my own land, Tír na nÓg,' she responded. 'And now it is your land, too. In it you will find everything I promised you.'

The white steed landed near the palace and Niamh and Oisín dismounted. A troop of tall warriors marched from the palace and, drawing up in front of them, they saluted ceremoniously.

These were followed by a group of nobles, led by the king, who wore a blue satin robe covered with precious gems and a golden crown sparkling with diamonds. Next came the queen with her attendants, a hundred lovely young maidens. Never before had Oisín seen a king and queen so full of grace and majesty. They greeted their daughter and embraced her.

The king turned to Oisín and, offering him his hand, he said, 'A hundred thousand welcomes!' Then, turning to the others, he declared, 'This is Oisín, son of Fionn

Mac Cumhaill, the great leader of the brave Fianna in Ireland. He is to be the husband of our beloved daughter, Niamh Cinn Óir.'

Facing Oisín again, he laid his hand on his shoulder. 'You will never grow old in this magical land of ours,' he said. 'You will enjoy every kind of delight. My gentle daughter will be your wife and you will live happily together for ever and ever.'

Oisín thanked the king and bowed to the queen. They went into the palace, where a great banquet had been prepared in their honour. The feasting and celebration went on for ten days. On the tenth day, Oisín was married to Niamh of the Golden Hair.

For many years they lived happily together in Tír na nÓg. Time passed so quickly in this magical land that to Oisín it seemed like only a short period since he had left his father and all his comrades in Ireland. Life was so peaceful that he had no need for his old weapons of battle and he put them away. His great sword he hung on the wall beside his bed, to remind him of his warrior days in Ireland.

One morning, when the rising sun turned the blade into a shaft of gold, he remembered guiltily his promise to his father. He took down the sword and held it out before him. As he began to recall all the adventures he had with Fionn and the Fianna, a great longing grew in him to go back to Ireland. He wanted to meet Fionn and his old comrades again and to sit around their camp fire talking about their latest exploits and hunting expeditions.

That evening, as he and Niamh were strolling in the grounds of the palace, he told her of his desire to return to Ireland.

A shadow passed over Niamh's beautiful face. 'Are you not happy here in Tír na nÓg?' she asked.

'Of course I am,' he assured her, 'very happy.' 'But I promised my father that I would see him again and I have never gone back on a promise. I shall not stay long there, Niamh. And when I come back I will never leave your side again.'

'Do you know how long it is since you left Ireland?' Niamh enquired.

'Two or three years?' Oisin guessed.

Niamh shook her head. 'It may seem like that here. But in the world you left behind three hundred years have passed.'

Oisín stopped and gripped Niamh's arm. The blood drained from his face.

'Three hundred years!' he gasped.

'Yes. And in that time many things have changed. Your father and the Fianna have passed on. A new religion has come to Ireland and has many followers. The old beliefs have almost died away.'

'My father gone? And the Fianna, too? I do not believe it!' Oisín declared. 'You are telling me these things to keep me from going.'

'I would never lie to you, Oisín,' Niamh said sadly, tears brimming over in her green eyes. 'But I can see that you will not believe until you have seen it for yourself.

Very well, take the white steed and go back to Ireland. But remember one thing: while you are there you must not get off the horse under any circumstances.'

'Why?'

'Because if even one of your feet touches the soil of Ireland you will be unable to come back to me or to Tír na nÓg ever again.' She took his hand in hers. 'And that would break my heart.'

Oisín kissed her gently. 'I give you my solemn promise,' he declared. 'I will return.'

❋   ❋   ❋

Oisín mounted the white steed and set off. The horse galloped towards the shore and launched itself over the waves. They travelled so swiftly that they outsped the wind and soon the green land of Ireland came into view.

The steed glided down and cantered through the country. Oisín looked carefully at every place they passed for any signs of recognition. It seemed to him that many things had changed since he was last in Ireland. Even in what used to be the Fianna's old haunts, places where they had hunted and feasted, he saw no trace of his father or of his former comrades. Gradually he began to fear that Niamh's information was true. His father and the Fianna had vanished from the face of the land.

As the steed galloped on, Oisín saw a group of men and women ahead. To his eyes they appeared to be very small and stunted, nothing like his own great size or that of the other members of the Fianna. He drew level with them and greeted them. They responded courteously, although they were clearly overawed by his appearance.

'Do you know anything about the whereabouts of Fionn Mac Cumhaill and the Fianna?' he asked.

They looked at one another in puzzlement. Then an old man stepped forward and said, 'We have indeed heard of the great Fionn Mac Cumhaill and the band of heroic warriors called the Fianna. Many stories are told about them and their wonderful deeds.' He shook his head slowly. 'But they lived hundreds of years ago and they are long dead.'

He looked at the powerful young stranger who seemed so affected by what he had said. 'According to the stories,' he added, 'Fionn had a son named Oisín who went with a lovely maiden to a magical land called Tír na nÓg. He was never seen again and his father and his friends were said to be very sad after his departure.'

With a heavy heart, Oisín set off on the white steed for the Hill of Allen where the great fort of the Fianna stood. Surely there, of all places, he would find the answers he was looking for.

The Hill of Allen was lonely and deserted. All that was left of the imposing fort which had once resounded with the shouts of warriors, the songs of bards and the happy sounds of people feasting and making merry was a crumbling ruin, overgrown with weeds.

Desolate, Oisín resumed his journey. He travelled on towards the east and arrived at a spot called Glenasmole, the Glen of the Thrushes. In the old days he and Fionn had often gone hunting there. He noticed a group of people gathered around something in the centre of the glen.

One of them called out to him, 'You appear to be a man of great strength. Please help us.' Oisín guided his horse over to the group and saw they were trying to raise a very large flat stone.

It was already half-lifted from the ground but the men beneath it were unable to raise it any further and were now trapped under its weight. They were in danger of being crushed to death by the stone.

Oisín could not understand why a whole group of men lacked the strength to lift a stone which he or Fionn or Oscar would have had no trouble in raising with one hand. Reaching down from his horse, he caught the stone with his right hand and prepared to throw it clear.

But, unnoticed by Oisín, the saddle-girth had loosened under the tremendous strain as he leaned forward to lift the stone, and now it suddenly snapped. Oisín was pitched sideways. Remembering Niamh's warning, he grabbed desperately for the reins, but they slipped through his sweating palms and he hit the ground. As soon as his right foot touched the soil a terrible change came over his body. The onlookers were horror-struck as, before their eyes, the mighty warrior – young, vibrant and strong – was reduced to a stooped, half-blind old man, his face seamed and furrowed with wrinkles and his muscled arms withered and shaking.

As soon as the white steed lost its rider it took off like the wind back to Tír na nÓg and was never seen again.

Seeing how weak he had become, and afraid to have Oisín among them after what had happened, the people thought it best to bring him to Saint Patrick. The saint took in the old man and gave him food and shelter for the short time he had left to live. As they sat around the fire at night, Patrick told Oisín all about the new faith he had brought to Ireland.

In return, Oisín recounted the many adventures of Fionn and the Fianna and his own stay in the magical world of Tír na nÓg.

And, on his deathbed, he dreamed that a lovely young girl on a white horse came to carry him off. It was his beautiful Niamh Cinn Óir, coming to reclaim the last of the Fianna.

AÍLNE'S REVENGE

The Fenian warrior patrolling the southern shore of the mighty River Shannon stopped and rubbed his eyes. He focused them again quickly and stared out across the broad expanse of water.

What he saw confirmed that he wasn't imagining things. A large fleet of ships stretched across the horizon, forty, maybe fifty of them. Their masts were hung with black raven flags which flapped menacingly in the stiff breeze as they sailed up the estuary towards the Kerry coast.

The warrior turned and raced away at high speed, his flying feet barely touching the ground as he ran. He must warn Fionn and the Fianna of this invasion as soon as possible.

Their billowing sails propelled by the strong wind, the ships headed swiftly for land and were soon anchored in a safe harbour. First to step ashore was the King of Iceland,

Mergach of the Sharp Spears. He was followed by a vast army of fierce-looking warriors, all armed to the teeth.

Mergach stood on a hillock and addressed his men: 'As you know, I have long wanted to add the land of Ireland to my kingdom. At last the chance has come. We have had fair winds behind us and the gods are with us. I swear to you, before the sun sets three times, Ireland will be mine!' He swept his arm towards the empty country-side behind him. 'No one stands in our way. Onward to victory!'

'Victory, victory!' With a mighty cheer the warriors echoed their king's battle-cry, raising their spears to the heavens in salute. Then, ranged into battalions, each under the command of a chieftain, they marched southwards towards their enemy.

For two days they met no opposition. On the third day, as they neared the top of a hill, a great force of Fianna warriors, led by Fionn Mac Cumhaill, swept down sud-denly upon them. A fierce battle raged for two days and two nights. Warrior stood against warrior in single com-bat and the clash of blade upon blade could be heard for miles around. When at last the fighting ended, Mergach, King of Iceland, and his entire army lay dead upon the battlefield. So great was the carnage that the hill on which they fought was known ever after as Cnoc an Áir, the Hill of the Slaughter.

When news of Mergach's death reached Iceland, his wife, Ailne, raised a great cry of grief and despair. 'By all the gods,' she swore, 'Fionn Mac Cumhaill and the Fianna will pay dearly for my husband's lost life.' Her brother, Draoiantóir, a giant and magician, also vowed to take revenge. His two sons had been among those slain in the bloody battle of Cnoc an Áir.

Ailne and her brother met in his castle to plan the best way to trap Fionn and his comrades. 'They are reputed to be very powerful warriors,' Ailne said. 'If they could overcome my husband and his army, no mortal power will be of use to us. You will have to use your strongest magic to capture them.' She drew closer to her brother and whispered: 'This is how I think we should do it ...'

❊   ❊   ❊

Fionn and some of the Fianna were hunting on the edge of a great wood. Suddenly, a deer came bounding out from a clump of bushes. For a second it paused in front of them, as though daring them to catch it, and then leapt away again.

It was one of the finest deer any of them had ever seen. Fionn signalled to his hounds, Bran and Sceolaing, and they set off in pursuit of the animal. Then he and his companions joined in the chase.

The deer sped like the wind over hills and glens. The hounds almost caught up with it a few times, but on each occasion, just as they were snapping at its heels, the deer put on an extra burst of speed and left dogs and men far behind.

Finally, it disappeared from view over a high hill. When the Fianna reached the summit, there was no sign of the deer anywhere. They broke into small groups and went in different directions in search of the animal. Fionn and Dara combed the small wood at the foot of the hill, but found no trace of the deer.

'The animal has got away,' Fionn said. 'There is no point in continuing with the search today. Let us return to our camp and try our luck again tomorrow.'

Fionn and Dara set off back the way they had come. But, without warning, a thick mist suddenly enveloped them. Unable to see further than a hand's breadth in front of them, they wandered off the track and stumbled into a clump of thorny bushes.

They decided to rest for a while until the mist had lifted. But, after some time, when there was no sign of any break in the blanket of fog, they began to fear that something was wrong.

'This is no normal mist,' Fionn said. 'I sense trickery. Let us sound the Dord Fianna, so our comrades will hear and come to our aid.'

The Dord Fianna was the traditional war-cry of the Fianna, which could also be sung in times of danger.

When their friends heard the Dord they knew that Fionn and Dara must be in some kind of trouble. Led by Oisín, they set off in the direction from which the cry came. But then the sound changed, seeming to come from a different location, and they turned around to head that way. Again and again the sound changed direction, until the warriors were left completely confused, calling out for Fionn as they raced this way and that.

Fionn and Dara could hear the shouts of the search party in the distance. But it was impossible to reach them through the dense mist. Then, close by, they heard a woman's voice calling. They groped their way out of the brambles into a clearing, where they almost fell over a beautiful young woman, slumped on the ground and looking very distressed.

'How do you come to be here alone in this forlorn place?' Fionn asked, gently lifting her to her feet.

'My husband and I were on our way to Tara when we heard the sound of hounds in chase,' she said. 'He went off to see the hunt, saying that he would return quickly. After waiting for a while I decided to follow him, but this terrible cloud came down and I lost my way.' Her voice broke on the last words, as she tried to hold back her tears.

'What is your name?' Fionn enquired.

'I am Glanluadh, and my husband is Lobharan.'

'My name is Fionn Mac Cumhaill, and this is Dara.'

'You must be the great leader of the Fianna!' the woman exclaimed. 'I am glad that I have met you, for I know that you will protect me and help me to find my husband again.'

'The Fianna are always glad to help a woman in distress,' Fionn said. 'But it will not be easy to find your husband in this fog that blinds us.' He smiled reassuringly. 'However, we will do our best.'

The three of them set off slowly, hoping to make their way into clearer air. They had gone only a short distance when they heard the sound of sweet music all around them. It was music such as none of them had ever heard before; it seeped into their heads and took over their senses. As the sound gradually grew louder they felt themselves becoming weak and drowsy. Their eyelids drooped and their knees buckled, until, finally, they sank to the ground in a deep and dreamless sleep.

When they woke up, the mist had disappeared. Fionn looked around and saw that they were lying on the edge of a big lake. The part nearest them narrowed to a channel. A large, many-towered castle stood on the shore directly opposite them.

As they stared across at the castle, two figures emerged through the gateway; a huge ugly giant and a pretty woman with a mass of auburn hair flowing over her shoulders. The two walked briskly to the lakeside and dived straight into the water. Swimming strongly, they quickly reached the side on which Fionn, Dara and Glanluadh were standing.

'I do not like the look of this pair,' Dara muttered as the giant and his companion strode towards them.

Fionn was about to greet them when the giant reached out with his huge hands, grasped the three of them by the neck, and frogmarched them down to the lakeshore.

Fionn and Dara were still too weak from the effects of the enchanted music to raise a finger to free themselves or Glanluadh. The giant and the woman jumped back into the water, hauled the three captives unceremoniously across the lake and tossed them up on the far side.

The giant shook Fionn until his teeth rattled in his head. 'At last I have you in my power, Fionn Mac Cumhaill! Soon my sister and I will have our revenge for all the suffering you and your treacherous Fianna have caused us.'

'You are mistaken,' Fionn protested. 'I have never seen you or your sister before in my life. How can I have caused either of you any harm?'

The giant gave Fionn another furious shake.'You lie!' he roared. 'I am Draoiantóir and this is my sister, Ailne. You treacherously killed her husband, Mergach, and my own two sons at the battle of Cnoc an Áir.'

'I remember that battle well,' Fionn said. 'I did not kill Mergach or anyone else through treacherous means. They were slain in fair combat. The Fianna have no need to kill by treachery.'

'I do not believe you!' the giant bellowed. 'You foully killed Mergach and my sons, and you and any other members of the Fianna that fall into my clutches will pay for that with your lives.'

The giant then dragged Fionn, Dara and Glanluadh into the castle. He pushed them down steep steps and, fixing chains tightly around their wrists and ankles, he flung them against the far wall of a dark, damp dungeon. 'You can rot here in the dungeon until I am ready to deal with you,' he snarled as he slammed the door behind him, leaving his captives shivering in the cold and wondering what dreadful fate awaited them.

❁   ❁   ❁

The other members of the Fianna were still searching desperately for Fionn and Dara. Although the mist had disappeared they could find no sign of the pair. The sound of the Dord Fianna had long since faded away. And even if they could still hear it they would no longer have trusted it, fearing that it would only lead them astray again. 'I think that Fionn and Dara have been spirited away by some magical spell,' Oisín said. 'In that case, they are in mortal danger. We must keep on searching.'

Oscar put his hand on his sword-hilt. 'And, if we find the magician who played this trick on us, we will make him sorry he ever heard of the Fianna!'

❁   ❁   ❁

A key rasped in the lock and the door to the dungeon creaked open. Ailne entered and stared down at Fionn, a gloating smile playing on her lips.

'Look now at the great Fionn Mac Cumhaill,' she mocked, 'lying there like a helpless infant!' She reached out and struck him across the face. 'Are you prepared to die?'

'We do not deserve this,' Fionn said quietly. 'It was wrong to deprive us of our strength by magical tricks and to throw us in this filthy hole without a morsel of food or a drop of water.'

'I have no pity for you!' Ailne hissed. 'I only wish that the rest of that band of murderers known as the Fianna were festering in this dungeon with you.'

'At least release this good woman, Glanluadh,' Fionn

pleaded. 'You can have no quarrel with her. She has no connection with me or the Fianna. She happened on us by chance when we were all lost in the mist. There is no reason why she should suffer with us.'

Ailne glanced at Glanluadh. 'Is this true?' Glanluadh nodded. 'I was travelling to Tara with my husband when I was caught in the fog and went astray.'

Ailne thought for a little while. 'Well, since you took no part in the deaths of my husband and nephews, you do not deserve my revenge. I am prepared to let you go.'

She released Glanluadh from her chains and led her out of the dungeon. The door was slammed tight and the key turned in the lock again. Fionn and Dara were left with their thoughts in the cold clammy darkness.

Ailne brought Glanluadh to the castle kitchen and gave her some food to eat. But Glanluadh was too weak to swallow anything and she collapsed to the floor. Ailne knelt beside her and put a golden drinking-horn filled with a pale liquid to her former captive's lips. As soon as Glanluadh had swallowed a few drops, all tiredness left her and she felt well and strong again. Springing to her feet, she thanked Ailne for her kindness.

'You are free to go now,' Ailne said.

'What will happen to Fionn and Dara?' Glanluadh asked.

'They will remain in the dungeon until it is time for them to die,' Ailne replied, with a grim smile.

Glanluadh dropped to her knees. 'Please let me bring them some food and drink before they die. Whatever they may have done to you, they protected me and showed me great kindness. Let me do this one thing for them before they are killed.'

'They will not be killed just yet,' Ailne said. 'My brother and I plan to use them as bait to lure other members of the Fianna here and complete our revenge.'

'All the more reason for giving them food and drink now,' Glanluadh urged. 'It will help to keep them alive until you have trapped their comrades.'

Ailne thought for a moment and then nodded. 'Very well, you may give them some food and drink, but I will be watching, so no tricks, or you will rejoin them, and this time I will not be so merciful.'

Accompanied by Ailne, Glanluadh returned to the dungeon with food and water. Fionn and Dara had grown even weaker. Glanluadh's heart was filled with pity, but Ailne stared down at them with a callous look on her face. She watched carefully as Glanluadh gave the food and drink to the prisoners.

They ate slowly but gulped the water down their parched throats. 'Enjoy the meal while you can,' Ailne sneered. 'It may be your last.'

❀   ❀   ❀

On the other side of the lake, the frantic search for Fionn and Dara was still going on, but, as time passed without any sighting, the Fianna were beginning to give up hope. Then there came an excited barking from Fionn's hounds, Bran and Sceolaing; they had picked up their master's scent. Straining at their leashes, the two dogs led the Fianna along a path which slanted down to the lake-shore.

The warriors stopped and stared across the narrow channel at the castle on the other side. Then, without hesitation, they plunged into the grey waters and swam across. As they approached the castle, Oisín ordered: 'Be ready with your weapons!' They drew their swords and went up to the castle gate.

Draoiantóir chuckled softly as he and Ailne watched from a tower high up in the castle. The Fianna warriors were walking straight into their trap! The giant slowly raised his hand; a bolt of blue light flew from his index finger and struck the group below. At once all the strength drained out of their bodies, and the warriors fell to the ground in an enchanted sleep.

Ailne and her brother ran down and dragged the helpless warriors into the castle. When he had shackled their arms and legs, Draoiantóir carried the prisoners down to the dungeon and flung them in beside Fionn and Dara.

'Now I shall take revenge on all of you for the deaths of my sons and Mergach!' he said, loosing his sword from the belt at his waist. Then a man's voice came from up-stairs, and Draoiantóir, fearing that he had been tricked, ran back up to confront the speaker.

A tall, dark-haired man was standing in the kitchen, talking to Ailne and Glanluadh.

'Who are you?' Draoiantóir demanded harshly.

'This is my husband, Lobharan,' Glanluadh replied. 'He heard the sound of the hounds and followed me here.'

Not believing her, and suspecting that Lobharan had come to help the Fianna, the giant grabbed hold of him and, despite Glanluadh's pleas, carried Lobharan down to the dungeon where he threw him in beside the others.

'I will make doubly sure that none of you can escape from here!' he said. Once more he extended his magical right hand and his prisoners found themselves fixed to the floor, unable to move a muscle.

'Whatever gods you pray to,' he said, 'pray to them now.' Draoiantóir drew his great sword and strode over to Conán Maol. 'I'll start with you, fat man!' he roared.

Although Conán Maol was always boasting about his bravery and his great prowess in battle, in reality he feared death more than anybody else. As the broad blade was raised over his head he was gripped with a terror greater than he had ever felt before. He heard a rushing in his head, the blood surged through his veins, and a strange and unnatural strength coursed into his body.

With a mighty leap, he rose high in the air, evading the blow from the giant's sword. But, in doing so, he left the skin from his back behind him on the floor. The furious giant followed him with upraised sword. 'You shall not escape me again!' he roared.

'Wait!' Conán cried out. 'Look at how injured I am.' He turned to show his back, which was bleeding and raw from neck to waist. 'Let me die of my wounds.'

The giant hesitated and slowly lowered his sword. He laughed evilly. 'A slow death is a painful death. Yes, I will leave you to die slowly in front of your friends. Your screams will make them suffer all the more. Then, when you have met your wretched end, I will send them to theirs.' He stamped out and locked the door.

Lobharan looked at Fionn who was lying near him. 'Glanluadh told me that there is a magical drinking-horn upstairs in the kitchen. If we could drink from that, it would free us from whatever spell is upon us.'

Fionn shook his head gloomily. 'If only we could reach it … but I can see no way of getting out of this dungeon.'

Oisín and the others agreed. Their feet and hands were chained, their strength had been drained from them, and the magician's spell had bound them to the floor. Despite their best efforts, they could do nothing.

Conán was the only one who had some strength, and, in spite of his injuries, he resolved to try and get a drink from the drinking-horn. But first he would have to outwit the giant. Each person in the group came up with a plan but someone else always had a reason why it wouldn't succeed. It seemed impossible.

At last they heard the key being turned in the lock and Draoiantóir clumped in, his sword in his hand. He went over to Conán and stared down at him.

'Are you not dead yet?' he growled. 'I am tired of this waiting.' He raised his sword high over Conán's head.

Conán held up his hand and spoke. 'Well,' he said,

'what a great feat it will be, to kill a man already mortally wounded! Is it the custom in Iceland to kill those who are already dying? What kind of honour is that? You accused us of foully murdering your sons, but now you plan to avenge their honourable deaths by this shameful deed. When they talk of this day by the fires in years to come, the storyteller will recount how the mighty magician, Draoiantóir, bravely killed Conán Mac Morna, a fat, bald defenceless man, wounded and hardly able to stand!'

Conán laughed. 'Oh, your name will be remembered, all right, Draoiantóir, remembered as a coward.'

'A coward? How dare you call me a coward!' the giant roared in a voice like thunder and his face turned so red it looked as though he was about to explode.

'Well,' Conán replied, 'if you are not a coward then make me whole again and we will see how brave you are confronting a warrior of the Fianna in all his powers.'

'Ailne!' Draoiantóir yelled up the stairs. 'Bring me the drinking-horn.'

Conán's eyes lit up with hope when he heard Ailne's footsteps on the stone stairs. But they clouded again in disappointment when he saw that she carried not the magical drinking-horn he had expected, but a large woolly sheepskin.

'Put this on his back,' Ailne instructed her brother. Draoiantóir took the sheepskin and placed it firmly on Conán's raw back. His wounds were instantly healed.

'Now,' Ailne said, 'kill him!'

The giant raised his sword and advanced on Conán.

The great blade flashed down with deadly purpose. Then, at the last second, Draoiantóir jerked back and the blade whistled harmlessly past Conán's left shoulder.

No one was more surprised than Conán to find that he still had his head. With both hands he felt around his neck as though only by touching the muscle and skin could he really believe that he was still alive. Finally, he looked at the giant, his face a mixture of relief and suspicion. 'What kind of cruel trick is this?' he asked.

'Trick?' the magician replied. 'You are the one with the tricks. I see your plan now. You fooled me into healing your wounds so that I would give you the honourable death you desired. But I'm not going to. I am going to make you my slave. We will see how a Fianna warrior enjoys being a lowly servant!' His lips twisted in an evil grin.

'No! Kill him now!' Ailne screamed.

'Not until I have had my fun with him,' Draoiantóir insisted. He shrugged his shoulders. 'I can always chop his head off if I find that he is not satisfactory.'

Ailne stamped her foot in fury and ran from the dungeon. The giant called to Conán to follow him upstairs.

Fionn could not believe it when he saw Conán obey the magician. How could he willingly serve an enemy of the Fianna? Where was his honour? He was about to shout out a reprimand to Conán, but he thought it would be best not to provoke the giant further while he and his comrades still had their heads on their shoulders.

Conán stopped at the top of the stairs and gasped like a bellows to get more breath into his lungs.

The giant turned and glared at him. 'Hurry up!'

'Although my wounds are healed,' Conán said to him, 'I am still very weak from the spell you put on me and my former comrades. I cannot work hard for you unless you free me from the enchantment.'

'I will give you a drink from the golden drinking-horn,' Draoiantóir said. 'Then you will be strong enough to carry out the duties of ten servants.'

They went into the kitchen where Glanluadh and Ailne were sitting. Glanluadh looked up fearfully, afraid of what news the giant might bring about the fate of her husband and the other captives. 'Hand me the drinking-horn,' Draoiantóir said to his sister. 'This slave of mine is still weak from the spell and a drink from it will restore his strength.'

'Is that wise?' Ailne asked. 'I shall not feel safe with a member of the Fianna about the place.'

'He is no longer one of that treacherous band,' the giant declared. 'He serves me now. As for the others, I shall go back and slay them all as soon as I have removed the spell from my servant.'

'The sooner the better,' Ailne smiled. 'I shall feel a lot happier when you have finally chopped off their heads.'

She gave the drinking-horn to her brother, who handed it to Conán. 'Drink!' the giant ordered.

Conán took a deep draught of the golden liquid from the horn and was instantly restored to his full strength.

❁ ❁ ❁

Down in the dungeon, Dara, who had a very fine melodious voice, began to sing one of Fionn's favourite songs, in order to raise his leader's spirits.

Draoiantóir heard the sweet music from below. Enchanted by the sound, the giant moved to the open door, forgetting that Conán still held the magical drinking-horn. As if in a trance, Draoiantóir moved down the stairs towards the source of the singing.

Conán saw his chance. He turned his back on Ailne and hid the drinking-horn under his tunic. 'I had better follow my master,' he said, leaving the kitchen and going down to the dungeon.

He moved quietly through the open door and stood behind Draoiantóir, who was listening intently to Dara's song. Conán sneezed suddenly and the giant swung around.

'What are you doing here?' he demanded.

'I came to see my former comrades before you put them to death,' Conán replied.

The giant eyed him suspiciously. 'What did you do with the drinking-horn?'

'I left it in the kitchen,' Conán lied.

Draoiantóir pushed him aside and rushed up the stairs.

Conán pulled the drinking-horn from under his tunic and held it to the lips of Fionn and the others. They drank from the horn and the strength flooded back into their bodies. As their muscles bulged, the chains fell from their limbs and they began to look around for their weapons.

But only Oscar had time to seize his spear and sword before the giant stormed back into the dungeon. Ailne and Glanluadh followed him and paused at the door.

'You deceived me, you treacherous dog!' Draoiantóir snarled. With upraised sword he rushed at Conán, who jumped aside as the great blade whistled past his head.

'Save me, Oscar!' Conán yelled.

Oscar leapt to cover his comrade, and, with both hands grasping his spear, he aimed its deadly tip at the giant.

Draoiantóir bared his teeth in a vicious grin. 'I shall kill you first, you Fianna whelp! Then I shall slice the heads off the others.'

He swung his sword at Oscar's neck. Fionn's grandson dodged the blow and quickly jabbed his long spear into the magician's arm. The giant bellowed in a mixture of pain and anger. He launched a fierce attack and drove Oscar back towards the far wall of the dungeon. Oscar caught his heel on a discarded shackle. Thrown off balance, he stumbled and Draoiantóir closed in on him, his sword poised for the kill.

But Oscar recovered his footing and, as Draoiantóir prepared to deliver the fatal blow, the Fianna warrior slipped under his arm and plunged his spear into the giant's heart. Draoiantóir gasped and slid to the ground, fatally wounded. When Ailne saw her brother's lifeless body, she let out one piercing scream and fell dead on the floor.

Moved by pity, Glanluadh knelt by Ailne's body.

'Waste no tears on her or her brother,' Conán advised. 'They were evil people who would have killed us all, your own husband included.'

'It is over,' Fionn said. 'Let us celebrate our narrow escape from death.' With Glanluadh and her husband, he and his comrades went upstairs, where Conán lost no time in collecting plates of delicious food and bowls of the finest mead.

Fionn proposed a toast. 'To Conán, the hero!' They drank in Conán's honour and the warrior stood on the table to receive their praise.

'You can take off that sheepskin now,' Fionn told him, 'else the dogs will take to herding you for a sheep.' The others all laughed.

But, try as he might, Conán could not tear off the sheepskin covering. And, for the rest of his life, that sheepskin remained stuck to his back. Every year the wool grew very thickly on it and he became known as Conán Maol of the Woolly Back!

The Fianna sang and danced until they were tired. That night they slept soundly on the castle's soft couches. When they woke up next morning the castle and the lake had disappeared. They found that they were now lying in the very same spot where they had first seen the deer, when out hunting.

Oscar glanced around. 'Where are Glanluadh and her husband?' he asked.

'Probably transported like us back to their own place,' Fionn surmised.

Conán rose and patted his stomach, which was grumbling noisily with hunger. 'I'm ravenous,' he groaned. 'Let's go back to our camp and have a good meal.'

Oscar's face broke into a broad smile. 'It looks as though everything is back to normal again,' he chuckled.

ALSO BY LIAM MAC UISTIN

THE HUNT FOR DIARMAID AND GRÁINNE

One of the Great Tales from the ancient Celtic tradition. This story tells of how Fionn Mac Cumhaill, the great Fianna leader, wishes to marry the beautiful Gráinne, but she will not have him. Instead she runs off with Diarmaid, a trusted member of the Fianna. Then begins the great chase in pursuit of the couple and the final battle, involving mixed loyalties, a warrior's honour and a woman's tragedy.

Paperback £3.99/€5.07/$7.95

THE TAIN

The most famous Irish legend of all in an exciting and easily understood version. Tells of the great battle between the famous warrior Cúchulainn and his closes friend, Ferdia. When these two heroes clash, the four shores of Ireland echo to the sound of their terrible battle.

Paperback £3.99/€5.07/$6.95

L 13

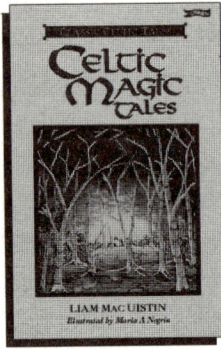

CELTIC MAGIC TALES

Four magical legends from Ireland's Celtic past vividly told – heroic quests, great deeds, fantasy and fun.

The rich lore of magic from the ancient Celts fills these stories of the love quest of Mir and Aideen, the adventure of the sons of Tuireann, the mischievous Bricriu and the famous love epic of Deirdre.

EXPLORING NEWGRANGE

Also from Liam Mac Uistin, this book explores the creation, building and discovery of Newgrange – one of the oldest burial sites in the world.

Send for our full-colour catalogue